I WISH I WAS THE BABY

By DJ Long

Illustrated by Gary Johnson

ideals children's books...
Nashville, Tennessee

First paperback edition printed in 2002.

ISBN 0-8249-5441-6

Published by Ideals Children's Books
An imprint of Ideals Publications
A division of Guideposts
535 Metroplex Drive, Suite 250
Nashville, Tennessee 37211
www.idealsbooks.com

Printed and bound in Mexico by R.R. Donnelley.

Library of Congress Cataloging-in-Publication Data:

Long, DJ.
I Wish I Was the Baby / DJ Long; [illustrated by] Gary Johnson.
  p.   cm.
Summary: Unhappy over the attention that his new baby sister
receives, a young boy dreams that he trades places with her and
discovers that he likes being the big brother better.
    [1. Babies—Fiction. 2. Brothers and sisters—Fiction. 3. Stories in
rhyme.] I. Johnson, Gary, ill. II. Title.
PZ8.3.L86194Iaw   1995
[E]—dc20   94-40664
                                        CIP
                                        AC

1 3 5 7 9 10 8 6 4 2

The day they brought the baby home,
They said I had a sister.
Then everybody stood around
And held and hugged and kissed her.

They brought a fluffy stuffy bear
Tied with a big pink bow,
And quite a pile of presents . . .
There were some for me, I know.

She got a cup, she got a dress,
Some shirts and lacy booties,
A blanket and a savings bond . . .
I got a box of Frooties.

The more the baby got, I thought,
The more that I could see
I wished I was the baby and
I wished that she was me.

They put the baby in my arms.
They said, "Now don't you drop her!"
She started squirming—I held tight.
She cried—I couldn't stop her.

"You poor thing," everybody said.
I thought they meant me, maybe.
I thought I'd get a hug, at least,
But they were hugging Baby.

They stuck a bottle in her mouth.
They tried a pacifier.
They rocked and walked and sang
        and talked . . .
My goodness, what a crier!

When finally things got quiet
And they put Baby away,
I thought it must be my turn now,
So I began to play.

I built a tower with my blocks,
But it came crashing down.
The baby woke *a little bit*,
And everybody frowned.

I put my engine on its track
Without a single sound,
And then I turned the engine on
To make it go around.

TOOT! TOOT! The train began to chug.
The baby! I forgot!
Everybody yelled at me . . .
The baby woke *a lot*.

I wished I was the baby
And had the baby's things,
The bottles and the blankets,
The buggies and the swings.

I wished I was all pink and small
As she lay tucked in bed.
I wished I was the baby,
And she was me instead.

The sun came shining in the room . . .
I opened up my eyes.
I took a look at Baby's bed
And got a big surprise.

The baby on my rocking horse—
She's wearing my new pants!
The baby putting on my tapes
And getting up to dance!

The baby on my potty chair
And washing in my sink!
Hey, something funny's going on.
Something strange, I think.

I try to get out of my bed—
I don't go anywhere.
That baby's using my blue comb
To comb her fuzzy hair!

I try to call my mother,
But I cannot say a word.
I hear myself just crying, "WAH!"
And hoping someone heard.

They come and change my diaper.
They come and tell me, "Hush."
But how can I be quiet?
Baby's got my new toothbrush!

They stick a bottle in my mouth—
The baby's got my spoon.
She's got my favorite cereal.
She's watching my cartoons.

The baby's going out to play.
She's talking with my friend.
The baby's got a green balloon . . .
My pants are wet again.

Now powder's getting in my nose
And smells I do not like.
They're putting me in Baby's clothes.
Hey! Baby's on my bike!

She's running, skipping, jumping—
I just wish that I could walk.
She's singing all my favorite songs,
And I can't even talk.

. . . "Wake up!" my mother calls.
"You are such a sleepyhead."
I open up one eye and look.
There's Baby in her bed.

I try—yes, I can get up now.
I slide out from the sheet.
So was I only dreaming?
Look! I'm walking on two feet!

I tiptoe to the baby's crib.
She's watching me, I see.
How glad I am she's Baby,
How happy I am me.

I show her pretty pictures.
I touch her fuzzy hair.
And maybe when she's older,
There'll be toys that we can share.

The diapers and the rattles—
They're for her, 'cause now I see
She's best at being Baby,
And I'm best at being me.